LETTER TO A LOST FUTURE

ABHRA BAPARY

Contents

1

Episode 1: The Bus Encounter

—♡—

I was traveling on a bus, returning from college. The day of spring always brings a chill, but this day felt different. How can you avoid feeling a bit warmer when someone of such beauty is sitting beside you? Her presence was captivating, and I could feel my heart beating faster. After some internal debate, I finally gathered the courage to speak to her.

Protagonist: "Hi, do you go to the same college?"

She looked up, slightly surprised, but then smiled. **Girl:** "Yes, I do. I'm in the final year."

Protagonist: "Really? I've never seen you before."

Girl: "I guess our paths just never crossed. I'm usually in the arts building. What about you?" **Protagonist:** "I'm in the science department. Maybe that's why. It's a big campus."

We continued talking, and I discovered she was from the same city as me and even lived in the same locality.

Protagonist: "That's a coincidence. Which area do you live in?"

Girl: "I live in the Lakeview Apartments. What about you?"

Protagonist: "I live just a few blocks away, in the Greenfield complex. It's a small world."

She smiled again, and we continued to chat. I learned that she was into painting and loved visiting art galleries. Her passion for art was evident and intriguing. But then, reality hit.

Protagonist: "I'm only in college on Sundays. It's a distance learning college for those who couldn't continue their regular studies, like me."

Girl: "Same here. I took up a job and couldn't manage regular classes."

A week-long wait followed. What could I do for those seven days? My mind was filled with thoughts of her. Every day seemed to drag on endlessly.

Protagonist (internally): "How will I survive until next Sunday? What if I never see her again? What should I say next time?"

The anticipation and hope of seeing her again were all that kept me going. The countdown to Sunday began, and with it, a glimmer of hope in my otherwise monotonous life

2

Episode 2: Pearl Diagnostic Centre

Monday arrived, and it was time for my counselling session. My mom and I headed to the Pearl Diagnostic Centre. This was my fifth session with Dr. Sikha Dey. Though I'd been to counselling before, this felt different. Dr. Sikha Dey greeted us with her usual warm smile.

Dr. Dey: "How are you doing today?"

Protagonist: "Just trying to do better."

Dr. Dey: "Good boy. Mrs. Sarkar, can you step outside? I'd like to talk with him alone."

My mom left the room, and Dr.Dey focused her attention entirely on me.

Dr. Dey: "So, how are things going? Any changes?"

Protagonist: "Same as always. No change."

Dr. Dey: "Don't be so sure. Change takes time. You've just started this journey. There are already differences between your first day and today."

She paused before continuing with a more serious tone.

Dr. Dey: "I've heard you're spending a lot of time in bed. Don't you want to feel better? You say you do, but you have to make an effort. Leave the bed early, go outside."

Protagonist: "Why should I? I have no friends, no girlfriend. I'm not good at sports or anything."

Dr. Dey: "There are other things you can do. Play chess, read books, or write something. I've heard you're good at writing. Stories, poems—why not write your feelings and problems in story format? It can be therapeutic."

I looked at her, skeptical but willing to try anything.

Protagonist: "But these problems feel unsolvable."

Dr. Dey: "How do you know that? You can't give up so easily. Go through the process. Don't expect results overnight."

Protagonist: "You told me to write, but I don't have anyone to listen."

Dr. Dey: "What about your sister? What about Your mom?"

Protagonist: "They're busy with their own things."

Dr. Dey: "Ask them. They can still make time for you. Writing can be powerful, but sharing it with someone can be even more so."

Protagonist: "Okay, I'll try writing my story."

Dr. Dey: "Good boy. Go ask your mother to come in."

I went outside and called my mom back into the room.

Protagonist: "Mom, Dr. Dey wants to see you again."

Mrs. Sarkar: "Yes, what is it?" **Dr. Dey:** "Mrs. Sarkar, I've suggested your son start writing to work through his feelings. It's important for him to feel supported at home. If you could listen to his writings and give him some time, it would make a difference."

Mrs. Sarkar: "I'll try to be more involved. It's been difficult with everything going on."

Dr. Dey: "Thank you. Your support is crucial. We'll review his progress in our next session." **Protagonist:** "I'll give it a shot, but I'm not sure how much it will help."

Dr. Dey: "That's a start. Keep up the effort, and we'll see how it goes." Leaving the session, I felt a mix of hope and doubt. Could writing really change anything? Only time would tell.

3

Episode 3: The Secret of My Life

Everything doesn't last long, just like my fleeting moments of happiness. The next day morning, it's all the same. Noon is my morning. I wake up at 12:00 PM, sometimes brush my teeth, sometimes not. I go through the motions of morning tasks, then return to bed with my mobile phone. I play games, eat junk food in the evening, start surfing on YouTube, and then go back to sleep. How gloomy is that? How did it all start? I left my college behind, and with it, any future I had envisioned. I lost my feelings in conversations with others and ended up hurt many times. Befriending people only led me to believe that friendship isn't for me. I couldn't continue my studies and, overwhelmed by anxiety, opted for Sunday classes—just a couple of hours of interaction a week. I'm an ambivert, struggling with behavioural problems. Maintaining connections and finding a sense of purpose has always been a challenge. My days have become monotonous, filled with long hours of sleep, mobile games, and avoidance of meaningful activities. It feels like I'm existing rather than living, trapped in a cycle that I can't seem to break.

4

Episode 4: The New Week at College

Monday arrived, bringing me back to college. The stark contrast between the vibrant campus atmosphere and my monotonous routine felt more pronounced than ever. The day was abuzz with activity, yet my mind was consumed with thoughts of the girl from the bus.

Protagonist (internally): "What if I see her today? What if she remembers me? What if she's just as eager to continue our conversation as I am?"

Despite my best efforts, I struggled to focus on my classes. My thoughts kept drifting back to our previous encounter, and the anticipation of seeing her again heightened my anxiety. The lively college environment only amplified my self-consciousness. As the day dragged on, doubt began to seep in. I questioned the significance of our last conversation and whether it had meant anything more than a fleeting moment.

Protagonist (internally): "What if she doesn't want to talk to me again? What if she's already forgotten about me? Am I setting myself up for disappointment?"

Classes finally ended, and I headed to my usual bus stop. My heart raced with a mix of excitement and apprehension as I hoped to see her again. When she arrived, I was both relieved and elated. We greeted each other warmly, and she seemed genuinely pleased to see me.

Girl: "Hey! I was hoping to see you today."

We took our seats on the bus, and our conversation resumed effortlessly. We talked about college life, our interests, and our aspirations. Despite lingering doubts, I found myself enjoying our time together. The conversation felt more natural, and a sense of connection began to grow.

Protagonist (internally): "Maybe this is going better than I thought. Maybe she is interested in getting to know me." As the bus ride ended, I felt a pang of regret that our time was so brief. We exchanged goodbyes and promised to meet again next Sunday.

Protagonist (internally): "This week turned out better than I expected. There's a glimmer of hope. Maybe things are starting to improve."

The rest of the week was infused with a renewed sense of purpose. Our interaction had provided a much-needed break from the monotony of my daily life, and I looked forward to our next meeting with cautious optimism.

5

Episode 5: Anticipation and Uncertainty

Monday arrived with the usual routine, but this time, the day felt different. The excitement and nervousness about our next meeting with the girl from the bus were palpable. I spent the day at college, trying to focus on classes while my mind was preoccupied with thoughts of her.

Protagonist (internally): "What if she doesn't remember me? What if she's not interested anymore? What if this whole thing was just a fleeting moment?" The anxiety was Intense. I couldn't help but imagine different scenarios and possible outcomes of our next interaction. Each possibility seemed to bring its own set of worries and doubts. 11 As the day progressed, I found myself lost in a haze of speculation. Every interaction with others felt superficial compared to the depth of my thoughts about her. I couldn't escape the nagging questions that plagued my mind.

Protagonist (internally): "Will she be as engaged in our conversation as she was before? What if I say something wrong and ruin everything? What if our meeting turns out to be awkward or uncomfortable?"

By the time I left college, the anticipation was almost overwhelming. The thought of our next encounter filled me with a mixture of hope and dread. I was eager to see her again, but the uncertainty of what might happen weighed heavily on me. Later that evening, I found myself staring at the blank page of my notebook, trying to channel my feelings into writing. But the task felt daunting. How could I capture the uncertainty and hope that seemed to define my feelings about her?

Protagonist (internally): "How do I write about something that I'm not even sure about? What if my feelings are just an illusion? What if nothing changes, and I'm left feeling disappointed again?"

The process of writing was fraught with the same doubts that had been consuming me all day. I wanted to express my anticipation and hopes, but the fear of the unknown made it difficult to commit to any one idea. As the week dragged on, my thoughts were consumed by the possibilities of what might happen next. The wait for Sunday felt like an eternity, and each day seemed to stretch endlessly.

Protagonist (internally): "Will this Sunday be different? Will it bring the answers I'm searching for, or will it just leave me with more questions? I can't predict the future, but I can't help but hope for something better."

As I went to bed, the uncertainty lingered. The future was filled with possibilities, both hopeful and daunting, and I was left wondering how things would unfold in our next meeting. The anticipation of the upcoming Sunday was both a beacon of hope and a source of anxiety, and I could only wait and see what the future would bring.

6
Episode 6: A Sad Reflection

Tuesday morning came, and I awoke to the usual routine—noon was my new morning. I stumbled out of bed and made my way to the kitchen, where I found my sister sitting at the desk, absorbed in reading something. As I approached, I saw that she was reading my recent writings.

Protagonist: "What are you doing with my stories?"

Sister: "I was just reading what you've written. I wanted to see what you've been working on."

Protagonist: "I thought I asked you not to read them. It's supposed to be private."

Sister: "I know, but Dr.Dey mentioned that you need support, and I wanted to understand what you're going through. It's important, isn't it?"

Her eyes scanned the pages, and then she looked up, a thoughtful expression on her face.

Sister: "You know, after reading this, I think there's something you might have missed. You mentioned the bus ride and meeting the girl. Maybe you should have changed your seat. If you had done that, things might have turned out differently. Maybe you could have had a happier interaction."

Her comment cut deeper than I expected. It wasn't just a suggestion; it was a reminder of my perceived failures and missed opportunities. The idea that a simple change could have led to a different, potentially better outcome made me feel like I had missed a crucial chance.

Protagonist: "What's the point of discussing that now? It's too late to change what happened. It's just more disappointment."

Sister: "I didn't mean to upset you. I just thought it might be worth considering. It's a way to think about how small changes can impact the outcome."

Her words echoed in my mind, and I couldn't shake the feeling of sadness. The notion that a small adjustment could have altered everything was a painful reminder of how often I felt stuck in regret. It wasn't just about the bus ride; it was about the broader sense of missed chances and unfulfilled potential.

She patted me on the back, saying, "Don't be negative; be positive."

She left.

Protagonist (internally): "If only I had been braver or more positive. Maybe things could have been different. But now, all I have is the weight of what could have been." The realization of my perceived shortcomings and missed opportunities weighed heavily on me throughout the day. I found it difficult to concentrate on anything, my thoughts consumed by the sadness of missed chances and the sense of being trapped in a cycle of regret. As the day ended, I felt a mixture of frustration and melancholy. The interaction with my sister had been meant to help, but it had instead reinforced my feelings of inadequacy. I was left with a deep sense of longing for a different past and a somber reflection on how small changes might have altered my present. With a heavy heart, I returned to my writing, now tinged with a deeper sense of sorrow. It became a way to grapple with my feelings of regret and to search for meaning in the aftermath of missed opportunities.

7

Episode 7: The Gloomy Sunday

—♡—

Sunday arrived with a thick, oppressive grayness hanging over the city. The drizzle outside seemed to seep into my mood, making the day feel as drab as my thoughts. I prepared for college, but my heart was heavy with the worry that today might not turn out as hoped.

Protagonist (internally): "What if she's not here today? What if today is just like every other day, filled with disappointment?"

The bus ride to college felt unusually long. I watched the raindrops race down the windows, my mind filled with anxious anticipation. As the bus pulled up to the college, I scanned the area, searching for a sign of her. But as I walked through the campus, it became increasingly clear that she wasn't around. I went through my usual routine, attending classes and trying to focus, but the empty seat beside me and the absence of our conversations weighed heavily on me.

Protagonist (internally): "Maybe she's just late. Or maybe she decided not to come today. What if she's lost interest?"

The hours dragged on, each class blending into the next. The college, usually bustling with activity, felt eerily quiet and unwelcoming. My usual routines felt meaningless without the small joy of our interactions to look forward to.

Protagonist (internally): "How did I let myself get so invested in something that might not even be there? What if this is just another reminder of how solitary my life is?"

After classes, I lingered at the bus stop, hoping for a glimpse of her as I waited for my ride home. But as the minutes ticked by, it became clear that she wasn't coming. The bus arrived, and I took my seat, feeling a deep sense of disappointment. The ride home was a quiet reflection of my mood. The gloomy weather outside seemed to reflect the emptiness I felt inside. The excitement and anticipation of the past weeks had been replaced by a hollow ache of unfulfilled expectations. Back at home, I tried to distract myself with my usual routine—playing games, watching videos, and avoiding deep thought. But the day's events lingered in my mind, making it hard to escape the sense of loss. As night fell, I lay in bed, the darkness of the room mirroring the heaviness in my heart. Sleep eventually came, but it was restless and filled with vivid dreams. In my dream, I found myself on the same bus from before. The familiar sights and sounds were all there, but something was different. I saw her, but she wasn't sitting beside me. Instead, there was an empty seat next to her, and I could hear my sister's voice echoing in my mind.

Sister (in the dream): "Maybe you should have changed your seat. If you had done that, things might have turned out differently."

I felt a surge of anxiety as I watched someone walk toward the vacant seat beside her. It was as if time was moving in slow motion. The person—me, but not quite—passed by the seat, choosing not to sit beside her. My heart raced, and I felt a deep pang of regret.

Protagonist (internally, in the dream): "I should have sat beside her. Why didn't I? Why is this happening? I'm in a dream, aren't I? This story isn't real. I need to wake up. Wake up..."

I felt trapped in the dream, overwhelmed by a sense of helplessness. The scene replayed in my mind, showing the missed opportunity again and again. The bus ride seemed endless, and my frustration grew with each passing moment. The dream felt like a cruel twist of fate, a manifestation of my deepest regrets and fears. I woke up in the middle of the night, drenched in sweat, with my heart pounding. The sense of loss and missed chances lingered, making it hard to shake off the dream's impact. As I lay there in the dark, the gloomy Sunday had left its mark on my subconscious. The night was long and filled with restless thoughts, and the weight of the dream only deepened my sense of sorrow. The search for meaning and resolution felt as elusive as ever, leaving me to face another day with the haunting echoes of what might have been.

8

Episode 8: The Counseling Session

♡

Monday came, and with it, the routine visit to the Pearl Diagnostic Centre for my counseling session with Dr.Sikha Dey. Despite the challenging week and the emotional turbulence, I was ready to discuss my recent experiences. Dr.Dey greeted me warmly as usual.

Dr.Dey: "Good to see you. How have things been since our last session?"

Protagonist: "It's been a tough week. I had a really disappointing Sunday and a dream that left me feeling more confused."

Dr.Dey: "Let's talk about it. What happened?"

I took a deep breath, trying to gather my thoughts. I recounted the disappointment of not seeing her at college and the unsettling dream where I kept missing opportunities. I hesitated, feeling the weight of my unspoken feelings about the missed chance with her.

Protagonist: "I've been reflecting a lot, trying to find some meaning in all this. But I've been struggling with this sense of missed opportunity, like I let something important slip away."

Dr.Dey listened attentively, her expression encouraging.

Dr.Dey: "It's normal to feel regret about missed opportunities. Sometimes, our thoughts about these situations can be overwhelming. What do you think this missed opportunity means for you?"

I shifted uncomfortably in my seat, reluctant to dive deeper into the specifics. The opportunity was more than just a missed chance; it felt like a significant part of my life that I was too scared to fully confront. I doubted anyone could truly help me with these feelings.

Protagonist: "I'm not sure. It feels like something that's more in my head than something I can actually talk about or change."

Dr.Dey: "It's okay to feel that way. Sometimes, these thoughts are difficult to articulate. The important thing is to acknowledge them and understand that it's a part of your process. You don't have to have all the answers right now."

Protagonist: "I just don't know if talking about it will make a difference. It feels like these feelings are too deep or too personal." Dr.Dey nodded empathetically.

Dr.Dey: "It's understandable to feel that way. It's often challenging to share our most vulnerable feelings. Remember, the goal of our sessions is to explore these feelings at your own pace. You don't have to force yourself to share everything right away."

We continued discussing other aspects of my life and strategies for managing my feelings. Dr.Dey encouraged me to keep writing and to focus on finding small ways to make positive changes in my daily routine. As the session came to an end, I felt a mix of relief and lingering uncertainty. Although I hadn't fully shared the depth of my feelings about the missed opportunity, I felt a bit more equipped to handle my emotions.

Protagonist: "Thank you, Dr.Dey. I appreciate your understanding."

Dr.Dey: "You're welcome. Remember, it's a journey. We'll take it one step at a time. Feel free to bring up anything you're ready to discuss in future sessions."

Leaving the clinic, I felt a tentative sense of hope. The counseling session had helped me reframe some of my thoughts, even if I hadn't fully addressed all of my concerns. I knew the road to understanding and healing would be gradual, and I was beginning to accept that some feelings might take time to fully confront.

9

Episode 9: Facing the Past

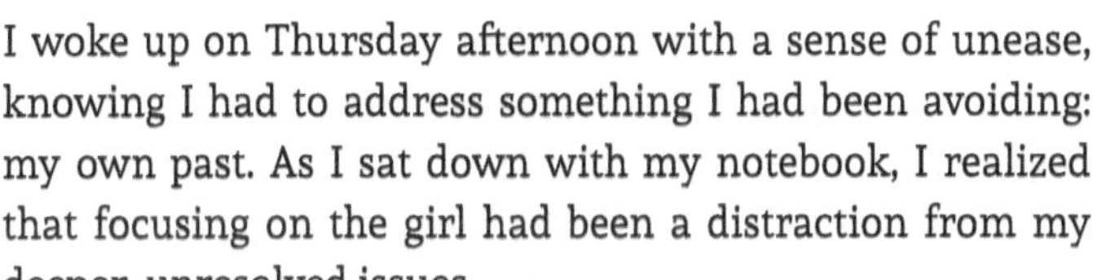

I woke up on Thursday afternoon with a sense of unease, knowing I had to address something I had been avoiding: my own past. As I sat down with my notebook, I realized that focusing on the girl had been a distraction from my deeper, unresolved issues.

Protagonist (internally): "Why have I been writing so much about her? I need to face my own life, my own history."

I began to write about my childhood and school years—moments marked by bullying, teasing, and mockery. These memories were painful and raw, reflecting a time when I was relentlessly targeted and made to feel inadequate.

Protagonist (internally): "The constant taunting and exclusion during school left scars that are still fresh. They made me question my worth and affected how I see myself."

As I wrote, I reflected on the naïve hope I had once held that things would get better with time. But the harsh reality of my past seemed to be an ever present shadow, influencing how I perceived myself and my interactions with others.

Protagonist (internally): "I thought innocence would be a shield, but it often felt like a weakness. The harshness of those experiences made me question everything I believed in."

The process of writing brought no comfort. Instead, it reinforced the depth of my unresolved pain. Each memory was a reminder of how those early experiences had shaped me, often leaving me feeling trapped and weighed down.

Protagonist (internally): "Despite my efforts to move forward, the impact of my past is still profound. It's like I'm stuck in a cycle of reflecting on what went wrong."

As the day progressed, I felt a growing sense of hopelessness. The act of confronting my past was both cathartic and painful, exposing the deep wounds that still lingered.

Protagonist (internally): "The more I write, the more I confront the reality of my sadness. The past continues to define me in ways I can't easily escape." By the time evening came, the weight of my reflections had left me feeling drained and defeated. I had hoped for clarity or resolution, but instead, I was left with a deeper understanding of the ongoing impact of my past.

Protagonist (internally): "I'm not sure if I've found any answers or if this will help me move forward. For now, it feels like the past is an inescapable part of who I am." As I closed my notebook, the sadness was palpable. I went to bed with a heavy heart, the reflections of the day echoing in my mind. The realization that my past continues to influence my present was a somber end to a day of deep introspection.

Protagonist (internally): "Tonight, the past feels as if it has the final word. The sadness of my history is overwhelming, and I'm left with the painful acknowledgment that moving forward won't be easy.

10

Episode 10: The Bonfire of the Past

The garage was cluttered with old papers, a collection of my past writings that I had been carrying for years. Among them were my stories, my thoughts, and the emotional outpourings that had become a part of my life. Now, with a sense of finality, I was determined to let go of the past. I dragged the stack of papers into the center of the garage and began piling them up. The act of burning these documents felt symbolic, a way to rid myself of the burdensome memories and the weight of unresolved feelings. As I struck the match and watched the flames flicker to life, I felt a mixture of relief and trepidation. The burning papers represented a symbolic end to a chapter of my life that had been filled with turmoil and introspection. The flames consumed the pages, and I stared at the fire, lost in thought. The crackling of the burning paper was both cathartic and unsettling. It was as if I was witnessing the destruction of a part of myself that I had carried for too long.

Suddenly, I heard footsteps approaching. My sister had walked into the garage and saw the fire burning in the center of the room. Her eyes widened in shock.

Sister: "What are you doing?!"

Her voice was filled with alarm, and she quickly ran to find our mother. I could hear her urgent footsteps as she left the garage, clearly distressed by what she had just witnessed.

Protagonist (internally): "I'm trying to let go, to move forward. But is this really the right way? What if it's not enough?"

As the flames grew larger, I felt a pang of regret. The decision to burn my writings was supposed to be liberating, but it was now causing a rift between me and my family. My sister's reaction made me question whether I had made a mistake. My mother appeared moments later, her expression a mix of confusion and concern.

Mother: "What on earth is going on here?"

Protagonist: "I just needed to let go of the past, to start fresh."

Mother: "This isn't the way to do it. You're upsetting your sister. We need to talk about this."

The conversation that followed was filled with tension and emotional weight. My mother tried to understand my motivations, but it was clear that my actions had caused a significant amount of worry and confusion. I felt torn between my desire to rid myself of the past and the consequences of my actions on those around me. As the fire finally died down and the last embers glowed in the garage, I was left with a sense of emptiness. The act of burning my writings had not brought the closure I had hoped for. Instead, it had created new conflicts and uncertainties.

Protagonist (internally): "Maybe I can't just burn away the past. Maybe it's not that easy. Maybe it will take more time to truly let go.

11

Episode 11: A Sunday Without Her

<hr>

The following Sunday arrived with a sense of quietude. With no college and no expectations of seeing her, it felt like just another day in a series of monotonous Sundays. The freedom from the usual routine was strangely disorienting. I awoke late in the afternoon, feeling disconnected from the usual anticipation that accompanied our meetings. The house was unusually quiet, and the absence of any plans or engagements left me with an unsettling emptiness.

Protagonist (internally): "Today is supposed to be a break, a day without the usual expectations. But it feels so empty, so devoid of purpose." I wandered around the house aimlessly, trying to distract myself with various activities. Despite my attempts to engage in different tasks, the absence of her presence was a constant reminder of the void I felt. The anticipation of our usual meeting had been replaced by a dull, oppressive silence.

Protagonist (internally): "Without the routine or the hope of seeing her, it's like there's a void in my life. The excitement is gone, replaced by a sense of emptiness." As the day wore on, I found myself reflecting on the events of the past week. The burning of my writings had left me feeling unresolved, and the absence of our meetings now seemed to magnify the sense of loss and confusion I felt. I spent the day in a state of melancholy, the weight of missed opportunities and unfulfilled expectations hanging over me. The house, once filled with the promise of a new week, now felt like a reminder of everything I was trying to escape from.

Protagonist (internally): "This Sunday is supposed to be a break from the usual, but it feels like a stark reminder of where I am now. The emptiness is overwhelming." As the evening approached, the reality of the situation settled in. The day had been filled with a sense of resignation, and I was left alone with my thoughts, grappling with the emotional aftermath of my recent actions and the absence of our meetings.

Protagonist (internally): "I thought this Sunday would be different, but it's just highlighted the emptiness I'm feeling. Maybe finding a new sense of purpose will take more time than I expected." The day ended with a somber reflection on the state of my life and the challenges I faced. The absence of her and the unresolved emotions from burning my writings had left me with a sense of uncertainty about the future.

12

Episode 12: The Session at Pearl and the New Beginning

Monday at Pearl Diagnostic Centre brought a mix of hope and trepidation.

Dr.Sikha Dey greeted me with her usual warmth as I walked into the counselling room.

'Dr.Dey:' How have you been? Any new insights or reflections since our last session?

Protagonist: "I've been working on understanding my past. I wrote about my childhood and the bullying I experienced.

"Dr. Dey:" That's a significant step. What did you discover through this process?

"Protagonist: "It was painful but enlightening. I realized how much my past has shaped my current feelings and why I escaped into fantasies. The girl on the bus was part of that escape.

"Dr. Dey:" Facing your past can be incredibly challenging. How are you coping with these realizations?

"Protagonist: "I burned my old writings, hoping it would help me move on, but it didn't bring the relief I expected. I also had a vivid dream about the girl, only to realize she was never really beside me—just an illusion."

Dr.Dey: "The process of letting go and facing reality is complex. It's normal to feel conflicted. Keep working through these feelings and give yourself time."

As I left the session, Dr.Dey's words lingered in my mind, offering both comfort and challenge. A profound realization began to dawn on me: the girl from the bus, the fantasies, the hopes—they were all illusions I had created to escape from the reality of my monotonous and painful existence.Walking back home, the weight of my realizations pressed heavily on me. The girl I had envisioned as a beacon of hope was never real. She was a figment of my imagination, a temporary distraction from the harsh truths of my life. The fantasy had only deepened my sense of isolation and despair. The effort to burn my old writings was supposed to symbolize a fresh start, but instead, it had exposed new conflicts and uncertainties. My sister's reaction and the subsequent argument with my mother highlighted how my attempt to let go had unintended consequences, further complicating my emotional state. By evening, the realization hit me with full force. My life, filled with moments of fantasy and attempts to escape, was unchanging. The girl was never a part of my reality; she was an illusion, and my efforts to escape my monotonous existence had led me to confront a painful truth.Yet, amidst the sadness, a new resolve began to form. I knew I had to find a way to address the reality of my life constructively. The following morning, I woke up with a reluctant acceptance. I decided to take practical steps towards change. I began by cleaning my room, clearing out clutter as a symbolic act of making space for a new beginning. I also returned to my writing, not as a means of escape, but to document my genuine feelings and aspirations.

Protagonist (internally): "This is a small start, but it's a step towards creating a new environment for myself. It's time to document my genuine experiences and aspirations."

As I engaged in these activities, I felt a tentative sense of hope. The journey of confronting my illusions and accepting reality was far from over, but taking these steps represented a commitment to facing my life with honesty and courage.

Protagonist (internally): "It's going to be a gradual process, but I'm starting to see that change is possible. I'm moving towards creating a new chapter in my life, one that is grounded in reality."

The night brought a sense of calm, and for the first time in a while, I felt that despite the challenges, there was potential for growth and transformation. The new beginning wasn't about forgetting the past but about finding a way to live meaningfully in the present and then life continues. Let see what challenges future brings.